Sneeze, Big BEAR, SNEEZE!

by Maureen Wright

illustrated by Will Hillenbrand

Marshall Cavendish Children

With love and pride to my husband, Don
—M.W.

To John Ertel, my first
art teacher and "aesthetic" father
—W.H.

Text copyright © 2011 by Maureen Wright
Illustrations copyright © 2011 by Will Hillenbrand

Marshall Cavendish Corporation, 99 White Plains Road, Tarrytown, NY 10591
www.marshallcavendish.us/kids

Library of Congress Cataloging-in-Publication Data

Wright, Maureen, 1961-
Sneeze, Big Bear, sneeze! / by Maureen Wright ; illustrated by Will
Hillenbrand. — 1st Marshall Cavendish ed.
p. cm.
Summary: Big Bear thinks that his tremendous sneezes are causing the
leaves and apples to fall off the trees and the geese to fly away, but when
the wind finally convinces him otherwise, he knows what to do.
ISBN 978-0-7614-5959-0 (hardcover) — ISBN 978-0-7614-6074-9 (ebook)
[1. Stories in rhyme. 2. Winds—Fiction. 3. Sneezing—Fiction. 4.
Bears—Fiction. 5. Autumn—Fiction.] I. Hillenbrand, Will, ill. II. Title.

The illustrations are rendered in mixed media.
Book design by Anahid Hamparian
Editor: Margery Cuyler

Printed in China (E)
First edition
1 3 5 6 4 2

mc Marshall Cavendish
Children

The wind whipped through the autumn woods
and swirled to the spot where Big Bear stood.
She whirled the leaves right off the trees,
just as Big Bear let out a sneeze.

The wind said, "Bear, can't you see?
The leaves flew down because of me."
Bear said, "Wind, it wasn't you—
the leaves fell down when I sneezed

ACHOO!"

Big Bear tried to nail the leaves back,
using a hammer and some tacks.

The wind kicked up and raced to the sky,
swinging down low, then spinning up high.
She said, "That bear knows nothing at all—
I dropped the leaves because it is fall!"

Big Bear walked as the cold wind blew
and came to a tree where apples grew.

Just as Big Bear let out a sneeze,
branches shook in a very strong breeze.

"Oh my!" said Bear with an unhappy frown,
watching the apples drop to the ground.
He knew as they fell with a thumping sound
that sneezing had made them all fall down.

The wind said, "Bear, can't you see?
The apples dropped because of me."
Bear said, "Wind, it wasn't you—
the apples fell when I sneezed

ACHOO!"

He put the apples on a branch of the tree,
stacking each one carefully.

The wind swirled 'round the forest glen,
dipping and whipping back again.
She said, "That bear knows nothing at all—
I dropped the apples because it is fall!"

Big Bear lumbered down to the lake.
Twenty geese rested, not one was awake.

Just as Big Bear let out a sneeze,
waves splashed up like a stormy sea.
The geese flew off with a honking sound,
flapping great wings above the ground.

"Oh my!" said Bear as he looked up high.
"What have I done?" he said with a sigh.

The wind said, "Bear, can't you see?
The geese headed south because of me."
Bear said, "Wind, it wasn't you—
the geese flew away when I sneezed

ACHOO!"

The wind spun 'round the autumn woods,
then circled back to where Bear stood.
She yelled, "Big Bear, I've had enough!
I'm tired of this crazy, ridiculous stuff."

Wind took a deep breath and let it out
with a whirling, twirling mighty shout—

"I WHIP THE LEAVES RIGHT OFF THE TREES

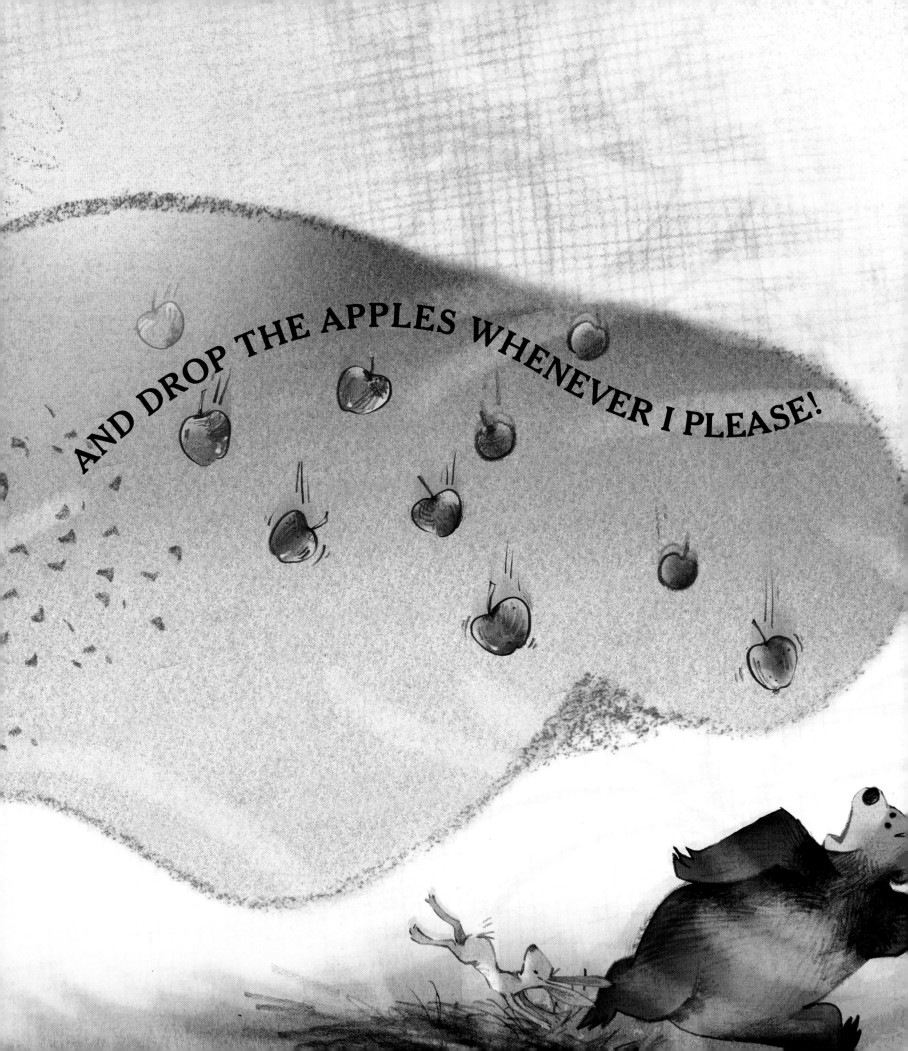

I SCARE OFF THE GEESE BEFORE THEY FREEZE

AND TICKLE YOUR NOSE TO MAKE YOU SNEEZE!

I DO IT ALL—
I'M THE AUTUMN BREEZE!"

Big Bear listened and scratched his head.
"You could have told me before," he said.
The wind's deep sigh shook the sky!

Bear said, "It's time to say good-bye!"

He ran to the safety of his den,
deep in the heart of the forest glen.
Suddenly the door slammed shut!
Big Bear's eyebrows shot right up.

He jumped in bed and covered his head
"I know my sneeze didn't do that!" he said.
"It's only the wind on a blustery night,
so, no more sneezes!" and he blew out the light.